High Jinks
the kids at Lincoln High

by
Debra Weiss

Watermill Press

Miss Bogda

Printed in the United States of America

Illustrations by Cat Calhoun

ISBN 0-89375-749-7

Contents

Shortstuff   5

Sideswipe   18

The Grind   32

Comeback   46

School Spirit   58

Best Friends   70

Why Can't You
   Be Like Your Brother?   84

Shortstuff

Mike Collins strained his neck until his Adam's apple stuck out and he could barely swallow. He rolled forward on the balls of his feet, lifting his heels off the scale. Coach Tanner scowled as he adjusted the metal measuring rod behind Mike's head.

"Stand still, Collins," Tanner barked.

Mike lost his balance. He fell backward onto his heels. "How can I measure your height? You're squirming and swaying all over the place. What's the matter with you?"

"I'm sorry, Coach. I was looking at something," Mike muttered under his breath. He was sure the other boys in the line were laughing at him. He kept his eyes glued to a poster of a baseball star on the locker room door.

"Mike was just stretching. He's going out for basketball this year, and he's got a little catching up to do before the tryouts," laughed Tom Johnson, the class loudmouth. Some of the boys snickered.

"Be quiet, Johnson, unless you want to run around the gym a few times to remind you to keep your mouth shut." The line fell quiet.

"That's, uh—five feet, three inches

even," the coach called out. His assistant, Joe, scribbled the numbers in a blue notebook.

"Are you sure it's not five-*four*?" Mike asked hopefully.

"No, it's definitely five-*three*," the coach replied. "But let me tell you something, Mike," he said gently. He leaned closer, so that the other boys couldn't hear. "Don't worry. I didn't get my growth spurt until I was seventeen. Then I just kept growing until I hit six-two. How old are you—fifteen, sixteen? You've got a lot of time!" He raised his voice and turned toward the other boys. "Next!"

"Thanks, Coach," Mike said, and he stepped off the scale. "I'll get you later, Johnson," he hissed as he passed Tom.

"So long, Shortstuff," Tom growled back.

Mike disappeared behind the lockers. He stuffed his gym clothes into his locker as fast as he could. In a few minutes, he had dressed, thrown his books into his knapsack, and slammed his way out of the locker room.

Tony Maslow, Mike's long-time friend, ran up to him. "Hey, Mike! What's the matter? You look really upset!"

"Listen, Tony, I can't talk here. I feel like I'm going to explode if I don't get out of here right now! Do you want to come outside with me?"

The two boys walked through the school yard toward Oakton Street. "That Tom Johnson really gets on my nerves," Mike began. "He's always calling me 'Shortstuff.' Today, he just went too far."

"I'm going to explode if I don't get out of here right now!"

"Aw, he's an idiot. Everyone knows it. Don't let him get to you."

"Well, it's not just Johnson," Mike said slowly. "But how could you understand?" he added bitterly. "You've got a great girl. Besides, you're . . ."

"I'm *what*?"

"You're *tall*," Mike said weakly. He was embarrassed.

"So you think your best friend doesn't understand, huh? You forget that I used to be pretty short myself until I grew six inches last year. Your turn will come."

"Have you taken a good look at my parents?" Mike asked. "I'm already much taller than my mother, and my dad's only a little taller than I am."

"Look, Mike, height isn't everything in this world. I think you're making too big a deal of this whole thing," Tony said. "Or is there something else on your mind?"

"There's something else, all right." Mike sighed heavily. "Do you know that girl, Nancy—the one with the really long red hair? I introduced you to her at lunch the other day."

"I remember her. Not bad. Not bad at all," Tony said slowly, giving Mike a sly look. "Why do you ask? Have you got a heavy date with her?"

"I *wish*," Mike said. He kicked a stone along the sidewalk. "You don't honestly think she'd go out with *me*, do you? People would laugh at her for being with such a shrimp! She's taller than I am, you know."

"No, I didn't know. If she is taller, it's not by much. *I* think you're about the same height," Tony replied.

"No, she's taller. If she wears heels,

11

forget it. I'd look like a fool. She'd either laugh at me or feel sorry for me."

"Mike, listen to me for a second. Don't you and Nancy always sit next to each other in English?"

"Yeah, so what?"

"And didn't she come over to you at lunch the other day?"

"Yeah, she sat at my table."

"And didn't you tell me that she asked if you two could study together for the midterm exam?"

"Yeah. So what are you getting at?"

"She's *interested*, Mike, that's what. You'd have to be a real dummy not to see that. But *she* won't make the first move, because she's not the type."

"How do you know so much all of a sudden?"

"I've got eyes. Besides, my girlfriend, Rhonda, knows Nancy from chorus, and she's *sure* that Nancy wants to go out with you."

Mike's eyes lit up. "Are you sure? Did Nancy actually say anything?"

"Some girls don't come right out and say things like that. They just *hint*. But Rhonda's sure," Tony said as he turned and walked up the driveway. "I'll see you tomorrow."

"I'll see you. And thanks, Tony."

The next morning, Mike was up much earlier than usual. He dressed very slowly, inspecting himself in the mirror every few seconds. *With these boots on, I must be at least five-five*, he thought. He ran his fingers through his hair until it stood up a little in the front. *Five*-six, he corrected himself.

Mike walked into English class with his heart pounding. He sat down in the back of the classroom and looked

Mike guided Nancy toward the other end of the hallway.

around. She wasn't there! Just as the bell rang, Nancy hurried in and slid into the empty seat next to Mike. "Boy, I didn't think I was going to make it!" she whispered, smiling at Mike.

"What are you doing after class?" he asked.

"Nothing special. I have a free period today." Nancy suddenly looked at her book and fell silent as the teacher scowled in her direction.

Mike passed her a note. "Do you have a minute to talk after class?"

"Sure," she answered.

The bell finally rang. Mike and Nancy walked out into the hall. "Let's get out of this crowd," Mike said. He guided Nancy toward the other end of the hallway. "Nancy," Mike began slowly, "we've been friends for a while now. I was just wondering if—"

A tall boy with sandy-colored hair burst in on Nancy and Mike. "Well, well, Red, I've been looking all over for you. Did you forget we had a date at 9:40?"

"Oh, Jack, I'm really sorry. I forgot all about it," Nancy said to the tall boy. Then she turned to Mike. "Listen, Mike, I can't talk right now. I'll see you at lunch — at the round table in the corner, OK?"

"Sure," Mike said. Nancy and the tall boy disappeared down the hallway. He had his arm around her!

Mike bought his lunch without even looking at the food. He forced himself to walk toward the corner of the cafeteria. Nancy was waiting for him! *But what's the use?* he thought. *She likes that tall kid. She'll never think of me as anything but a friend.*

Mike put his tray down on the table.

"Hi," he said, trying to smile.

"Hi. I was afraid you weren't going to come. I'm sorry about what happened before. You see, my cousin Jack just transferred to Lincoln High, and I promised I'd show him around today."

"Your *cousin*?" Mike asked in surprise.

"Yeah, he's like a brother to me. You didn't think . . ." Nancy giggled.

"Well, I'll be." Mike grinned. "Gee, I'm glad he's your cousin. Nancy," he said, pulling his chair closer, "would you like to go to the movies Saturday night?"

"I'd love to, Mike," Nancy said with a smile. "I guess you're not mad at me anymore?"

"No way!"

Sideswipe

Pat Blake pushed open the screen door and dropped her books on the kitchen counter. "Hi, Ma, I'm home!" she called out. She opened the refrigerator door and peered inside. "Mm, strawberries!"

"Pat, those are for dinner. I'm making strawberry shortcake for dessert," Mrs. Blake said as Pat popped a few into her mouth. "How was your day, honey?"

Pat poured herself a Coke and took a bag of potato chips out of the cupboard. "The math test was hard, but I think I passed, thanks to that cram session with Mary."

"Oh, Pat, you got a letter from the Motor Vehicle Bureau," Mrs. Blake said. She handed Pat an important-looking envelope. Pat opened it eagerly.

"It's my permit! I passed Driver's Ed, and I can take my driver's test any time after the first of May. Hey, that's today!" Pat hugged her mother. "Can you take me tomorrow? Please? After work? They're open till six."

"Let's see now. Tomorrow is Thursday. Yes, I can pick you up at 4:30. How's that?" Mrs. Blake smiled and sat down at the kitchen table. "Are you sure you feel ready?"

*Pat gave herself one last glance in
the hall mirror.*

"Oh, I'm sure. The longer I wait, the more nervous I'll get," Pat replied, and she reached for the bag of chips.

At 4:30 the next day, Pat was pacing up and down the front hallway. *I just have to pass this test*, she thought. *I've been waiting all year for this. Mary and Gayle will be so happy! I'll drive them over to Joe's for some pizza, and—*

Pat's thoughts were interrupted by a car horn. She could see her mother's blue Ford out front. She gave herself one last glance in the hall mirror. Then she grabbed her jacket and purse and went outside. She locked the front door with trembling fingers and joined her mother in the car.

"Hi, honey. All set?" Mrs. Blake asked.

"I...I guess so."

"You look a little pale, Pat. Are you sure you're all right?" her mother asked with concern.

"I'm OK, Ma, really. I'm just a little nervous, that's all." Pat tried to smile.

"OK, honey." Mrs. Blake pulled away from the curb. "Try to relax. You know you're a very good driver. The test will be easy for you."

Pat was very quiet all the way to the Motor Vehicle Bureau. Soon, she heard her mother saying, "Well, I've got to leave you here. I'll be waiting in there." Mrs. Blake pointed to a grey brick building next to the parking lot. "Good luck," she added. She kissed her daughter on the cheek. "Don't forget about the seat belt."

Mrs. Blake slammed the car door. Pat slid over to the driver's seat and strapped herself in. A grey-haired man with glasses and a plastic pin that read, "Mr. I.N. Sands, Instructor," walked over to the car and got in on the passenger side.

"Hello, young lady," he said. "May I see your permit, please?"

Pat gave it to him with shaking hands.

Mr. Sands looked at the permit and put it in his pocket. He fastened his seat belt. "All right, Miss Blake, just pull forward slowly until I tell you to stop."

"Yes, sir," Pat said in a small voice. She checked her side and rearview mirrors. Then she inched the car forward very slowly.

"Miss Blake," Mr. Sands said, clearing his throat, "I didn't mean *that* slowly."

"I'm sorry, sir," Pat said. She speeded up to twenty miles an hour.

"Now bring the car to a full stop and then back up."

Pat stopped the car and put it in reverse. With her foot on the brake, she checked both mirrors and looked over her right shoulder before backing up.

"That's fine. Now put the car in forward, and we'll continue."

Pat followed Mr. Sands' instructions. As the car approached a STOP sign, Pat came to a stop. She looked right and left to check for cross traffic. So far, so good. Maybe the test wouldn't be as bad as she'd thought.

Next, Mr. Sands told Pat to make a three-point turn and then a U-turn. She did both turns smoothly. Her confidence was coming back.

"Miss Blake, I want you to parallel park in the space between those two posts," Mr. Sands said. He pointed to an area by the right-hand curb.

Pat pulled up even with the far post. She backed slowly into the space. This was the part of the test she dreaded the most. If she touched the curb with her wheel, or parked too far from the curb, she'd fail the whole test. She straightened out the wheels and held her breath. Mr. Sands opened his door to measure the distance between the wheels and the curb.

"Well done, young lady," he said, closing his door. He was smiling! Pat breathed a sigh of relief. Now she was sure she would pass the test.

"If you'll just pull into the lot, Miss Blake, that will finish the test. I'll meet you at the front desk in a few minutes with your test results."

Pat spotted a space in the next row. She made a left turn and started to pull into the space. Suddenly, the car to her right backed up in her direction. "OH MY GOSH!" she cried. There was a loud scraping sound as the car sideswiped the passenger side of the blue Ford.

"What the heck is going on here?" Mr. Sands exclaimed. "Why don't you look where you're going?" he yelled out the window to the driver of the other car.

"Are you all right?" Pat asked Mr. Sands. She was fighting back tears.

"Yes, I'm all right. Turn the engine off and leave the car right here. We'll all have to go into the office and straighten this mess out." Mr. Sands got out of the car and inspected the damage. Pat also came around the car to look.

"Oh no!" she moaned. She caught sight of the long red streak on the side of the blue Ford. Mr. Sands was speaking to the other driver.

"Miss Blake," he said, nodding to Pat, "and Mr. Carlen," he said to the other driver, "will you follow me inside please?"

Pat's heart was pounding. Now she'd never get her license! And the car — how

"Are you all right?" Pat asked Mr. Sands.

would she ever pay for it? What would her mother say when she found out? She bit her lip hard to stop herself from crying.

Mrs. Blake was waiting inside the building. Mr. Sands spoke to her briefly. Then he turned toward Pat and Mr. Carlen. "Just wait in the office. I'll be out in a few minutes." He disappeared into a back room.

"Oh, Mom, I'm so sorry. I don't know how it happened. I was trying to be so careful," Pat sobbed, throwing her arms around her mother.

"Pat, it could have happened to anybody. The main thing is that you're all right," Mrs. Blake said, holding her tightly. "Thank heavens you're all right!" She glared at Mr. Carlen.

"Madam, I—I'm really sorry. I just didn't see your daughter until it was too late. It was my fault," Mr. Carlen said slowly. "Don't worry about the damage to your car. My insurance will cover that."

Pat blew her nose and wiped her eyes as Mr. Sands walked into the room. He cleared his throat.

"Miss Blake, I'm pleased to tell you that you have passed your driving test. You can pick up your license at the front desk," he began. Pat's mouth dropped open. "Mr. Carlen's insurance company has been told about the accident. His insurance will cover all damages, since the accident was Mr. Carlen's fault. I have a short form for you to fill out, and then you can go." Mr. Sands took off his glasses and rubbed his forehead.

"I passed, Mom! I can't believe it!" Pat whispered to her mother.

"She did a fine job, Mrs. Blake," Mr.

"I think I'd like you to drive this time."

Sands said with a smile.

"Well, would the new driver like to drive home?" Mrs. Blake asked Pat as she turned in the accident form.

"Ahh, I think I'd like you to drive this time," Pat replied, handing her mother the car keys.

The Grind

Ann Randall walked into the school cafeteria and looked for her best friend, Joanne Miles. As she took her place at the end of the lunch line, Sue West came up behind her.

"Ann, I've been looking all over for you! Have you got a minute to talk?"

"Sure, Sue," Ann said shyly. She

couldn't imagine why someone as popular as Sue would want to talk to her. Usually, Sue barely nodded to Ann when they saw each other in school.

"Let's eat lunch together, just the two of us, OK?" Sue asked sweetly.

"Well, I'd like to, but I'm waiting for someone," Ann replied, looking around again for Joanne.

"Who? Is it that girl with the glasses and curly hair—Jody something?"

"Joanne Miles," Ann corrected her.

"Look, if she's not here, she can't expect you to waste your whole lunch period waiting for her, can she?" Sue was leading Ann toward an empty table in the corner.

"She is awfully late," Ann said, as she eyed Sue's beautiful clothes and expensive haircut. She always felt so awkward and plain around Sue.

33

The two girls sat down and began to eat.

"Ugh, this is disgusting," Sue said, making a face. "I don't know why this dumb school doesn't let us go out for lunch. Have you ever been to Kenny's Place?"

"No, I haven't. Who is he?" asked Ann.

"Not *who*, silly. It's the name of a restaurant. Bill Riley took me there the other night. The food's out of this world! Not like this slop." She put her fork down. "Ann, I think we can help each other."

Ann stared at her in surprise. "How could I possibly—"

"Let me finish. Everyone knows that you're a real brain—especially in biology! Since we're in the same class, I thought you could help me." She lowered her voice and leaned closer to Ann. "If I fail one more biology test, I'm going to be off the cheerleading squad!"

"That's awful! Of course, I'll help you, Sue. I have a free period at 1:45 every day. If you want to study together—"

"That sounds good to me, but I might need some extra help after school once in a while."

"Any day but Tuesday or Thursday. I have to work those days."

"Thanks a million, Ann. I knew I could count on you. Now let me tell you how *I* can help *you*. I know a lot of great kids—especially *guys*. I'd like you to meet some of them. No one, not even you, can work all the time, right?"

"Sue, I don't think your friends would—"

"—like you? Don't be silly. Any friend of mine is a friend of theirs. I've got to run now, Ann. See you at 1:45 by the

"Listen, Ann, I really need to talk to you."

front staircase, OK?" Sue got up to leave.

"OK," said Ann, but Sue was already gone.

"Ann, where on earth have you been? I've been waiting for you for twenty minutes!" said Joanne Miles as she walked over to Ann's table.

"I waited for you, but you were late. Sue West wanted to talk to me for a minute, so I—"

"A minute! Lunch is almost over! Listen, Ann, I really need to talk to you. What are you doing during your free period?"

"I'm studying with Sue West."

"Studying? She never studies. Everyone knows she's a big cheater."

"She is *not* a cheater! I don't like to hear you talk about a friend of mine that way," Ann said angrily.

"Friend! You'll soon find out what kind

of friend *she* is. She uses people for all they're worth. Then she drops them like *that*." Joanne snapped her fingers.

"You always think the worst about people, Jo. But you're all wrong about Sue."

"No, I'm not. But I can see you don't believe me," Joanne said in a hurt voice. The bell rang, and Ann jumped to her feet.

"Oh no, I'm going to be late for my math exam! See you later, Jo?"

"After school?"

"OK, I'll see you!" Ann called as she disappeared through the doorway.

Ann and Joanne never did get to talk after school that day. Mr. Sommers, the biology teacher, announced that there would be an exam that Friday, and Sue begged Ann to help her study after school. She seemed so desperate that

Ann just couldn't say no. Sue didn't seem to know the first thing about biology. She borrowed all of Ann's lab write-ups to take home overnight. After they finished studying, Sue took Ann to the local hangout for a Coke.

Sue looked toward the door and smiled. "Well, if it isn't Bob and Bill Riley! Hey, over here!" she said, waving to them.

Ann felt herself getting goose bumps. The Riley brothers were stars on the school football team. They were in with the same crowd as Sue. No one that good-looking and popular would talk to her—she was sure of that. Before she could say anything, Sue introduced her to them as "my good friend Ann." They sat down next to the girls.

"Hi, Ann, nice to meet you. Where have you been all my life?" asked Bob. He moved a little closer to her.

"Watch out for that one. He's a fast mover," Sue said, winking at Bob.

"There you go again, Sue. You're ruining my reputation before I have a chance to do it myself!" Bob said with a loud laugh.

"I don't think you're so bad," Ann said with a smile. Maybe it wasn't so hard to talk to these guys after all.

"Hey, I think I'm going to like this girl," Bob said. He put his arm around Ann.

Ann was very happy. The next half-hour seemed to fly by. Bob and Bill drove her home in their silver sports car. "I'll see you tomorrow!" Ann shouted as they tore away from the curb.

At 1:45 the next day, Ann was waiting for Sue by the front staircase. Sue didn't show up until ten minutes after two.

"Where have you been? I've been

Bob and Bill drove her home in their silver sports car.

waiting for you for almost half an hour," Ann said angrily.

"Sorry, Ann, I just lost track of time. I was talking to Bob Riley. It seems he really likes you," Sue said sweetly.

Ann knew Sue was lying. Bob had passed her five minutes ago, walking in the opposite direction.

"Oh, really?" Ann said coolly. "I guess we'd better start studying. The period is almost over."

"Oh, Ann, I decided it's too late for me to catch up in biology."

"You mean you're not even going to *try* to pass?" Ann asked, surprised.

"No. With your help, I can still pass," Sue said in her sweetest voice.

"I don't understand," Ann said uneasily.

"All you have to do is sit on my left during the exam and let me copy your answers. Everyone does it." Sue shrugged. She didn't like the look on Ann's face. "Well, say something. Is it a deal?"

"Sue, that's cheating. I can't do it."

"Don't worry about getting caught. I know what I'm doing." Sue's voice rose as she realized that Ann was set against the idea. "Don't you care about our friendship? About Bob Riley? About the cheerleading squad?"

"I just can't do it, Sue. It's not honest. I'll help you in any other way, but not that. Please don't ask me to—"

"You'll regret this, Ann Randall! No one ever turns on me without paying for it! I'll see to it that Bob Riley never talks to you again! Go back to your stupid studying. Work, work, work—that's all you ever do. No wonder they call you 'The Grind!'"

*"Hi, Jo, it's Ann. Can we talk?
I'm really sorry...."*

Sue turned on her heel and walked out. Ann was stunned. She sank into a chair and was lost in thought until the bell rang. There was one thing she had to do right away.

As soon as she got home from school, Ann dialed Joanne's number. "Hi, Jo, it's Ann. Can we talk? I'm really sorry...."

Comeback

Jeff Reynolds was sweating heavily as he jumped down from the high bar. He could hardly breathe, and his shoulder was killing him. He wondered if he would ever be as good as he used to be—before the accident. He watched Mike Crane do a perfect back somersault off the bar. Jeff was the only one on the team who

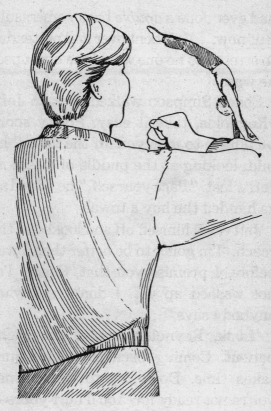

*He watched Mike Crane do a perfect back
somersault off the bar.*

had ever done a *double* back somersault. But now.... Jeff bent over and pretended to stretch so no one would see how upset he was.

Coach Simpson walked over to Jeff. "Reynolds, take it easy. Pretty soon, we'll have to mop you off the floor," he said, looking at the puddle of sweat at Jeff's feet. "Pace yourself," he added as he handed the boy a towel.

Jeff dried himself off and looked at the coach. "I'm going to be *better* than I was before. I promise you that, Coach. I'm not washed up yet. I don't care what anybody says."

"Look, Reynolds, you've got to be patient. Coming back from an injury takes time. Don't try to do routines you're not ready for. You'll hurt yourself so badly you'll never compete again. We don't want to lose you." He looked at

Jeff's red face and added, "That's all for today, Reynolds."

"OK, Coach. I guess you're right." Jeff looked down at his soggy sweat pants. "What I *really* need right now is a hot shower."

Jeff walked into the locker room and began to undress. It was one week until the meet against Madison High. This would be his first meet since the accident nearly six months ago. Somehow, in the middle of a big swing, he had lost his grip and gone flying off the bar. He landed flat on his back and was knocked out cold. The next thing he knew, he was in a hospital room with a broken shoulder blade and so many bruises that he couldn't move without feeling pain.

Even though Jeff was back on the team now, he still felt weak and out of shape. His shoulder hurt after a hard workout, and sometimes, he got dizzy. What was even worse, he was afraid. Every time he got on that bar, he could hear the gasp that went through the crowd when he fell. That was the last thing he had heard before he was knocked out. Jeff pushed these thoughts aside and slammed his locker.

Mike Crane was up ahead. He called out to Jeff. "Hey, Reynolds, do you want a ride? Baker's got the car."

"Sure, Crane, wait up," Jeff yelled after him, throwing his knapsack over his shoulder.

During the next week, Jeff worked very hard on his new high bar routine. He found it a little easier now, but he still had a long way to go. It was going to be a tough meet in more ways than one. Last year, before the accident, Jeff beat Madison High's top man on the high bar in a close meet. That contest gave the district championship to Jeff's school, Lincoln High. He knew that everyone would be watching him this time, testing the new Jeff Reynolds against the old one. Could he make a comeback?

The day of the meet, Jeff sat through his classes without hearing a word his teachers said. He saw himself flying around the high bar in perfect form until the very end of his routine. Then, all of a sudden, the bar slipped out of his hands. He was falling, falling....

"Reynolds, are you going to get on the bus, or do you plan to walk to the meet?" Coach Simpson shouted through the bus window.

Jeff shook off his worries and hurried onto the bus. Two doctors had told him that he'd never compete again. He'd show them. He'd show everyone. If only he didn't feel so shaky. He couldn't seem to get the accident out of his head.

"What's up, Jeff?" asked Mike Crane. He leaned over Jeff's seat. "You look as if someone just died or something. You know we're going to roast those Madison marshmallows!"

"Sure, I know. I was just thinking about my routine," Jeff said, forcing himself to smile. "Hey, we're here already," he added as the bus jerked to a stop.

An hour later, Jeff was waiting for his turn on the high bar. He kept wiping his hands so that they wouldn't slip on the bar, but his hands kept sweating anyway. He was next. Crane finished his routine with a beautiful back somersault and made a neat landing on the mat. As he passed Jeff, he whispered, "Go get them, Reynolds." Jeff smiled and gave Mike a "thumbs up" sign. Just then, he

"What's up, Jeff?" asked Mike Crane.

heard his name announced over the loud-speaker. This was it.

Jeff took a deep breath and stepped onto the mat. As his hands grasped the bar, he felt a thrill pass through him. It was so good to be back! He really felt *alive* again. He swung smoothly around the bar. For the first time since the accident, he felt confident with his routine. His timing and strength were coming back. Jeff swung around a final time and prepared to twist off the bar with a high spin in the air. But he misjudged the distance to the mat. He landed off balance. He quickly recovered, but he knew that he'd lose a few points for his sloppy landing.

As he took his final pose on the mat, the entire team from Lincoln High stood up and applauded. Jeff looked at them in amazement. Why were they clapping after that poor finish? As he walked back to the team, Coach Simpson came over to him. He was grinning from ear to ear as he slapped Jeff on the back.

"Great job, Reynolds! I knew you had the guts to do it!"

Jeff's teammates seemed to be all around him, cheering him on. Suddenly, there was a hush as the judges got ready to announce Jeff's score.

Jeff clenched his hands into fists and stared at the judges' board. The number was up now: 8.3. He was stunned. He'd never gotten below a 9.0. Before the accident, he got 9.5 and 9.6 at meets. *Some comeback,* he thought to himself.

The judges added up the final scores. Lincoln High won the meet! The whole team started cheering and yelling. Coach Simpson was yelling the loudest of them all. Then he caught sight of Jeff's tense,

"You'll get it, Reynolds—next time."

unhappy face. He made his way over to Jeff.

"Reynolds, we won! *All* of us together! And you were terrific. So why the long face?"

"I messed up, Coach. That landing..." Jeff looked at the floor.

"You'll get it, Reynolds—next time." The coach turned toward the rest of the team and shouted, "How about stopping at Joe's for some pizza? You boys earned it!"

A yell went up through the team.

"I'm starving," Jeff said to Mike as they walked outside to the bus. He was beginning to feel better already. "Hey, Coach," he shouted back to Simpson. "Next time for sure!"

School Spirit

Jill Palmer took a deep breath and walked back to the mat. *One more time,* she said to herself as she prepared to do a cartwheel.

"Jill, straighten those legs!" Coach Remick shouted.

Jill sighed. She had been working on cartwheels for weeks, but she still couldn't get her legs completely straight in the air. And cheerleading tryouts were tomorrow! She watched Liz Hanley do five cartwheels in a row. *Why can't I be as athletic as Liz? Some people have all the luck,* she thought.

Jill was a hard worker. She had lots of school spirit. But she just wasn't very athletic. Her friends tried to talk her out of trying out for the cheerleading squad. She wouldn't listen. Now she was beginning to fear that they were right.

Well, it's too late to quit now, she said to herself. *I'll just do the best I can, that's all.* She was the last one left in the gym that night. The coach was getting ready to lock up.

"Jill, it's time to go home!" she said. "Save some energy for the tryouts."

Jill picked up her sweat pants and headed toward the locker room. "Good

59

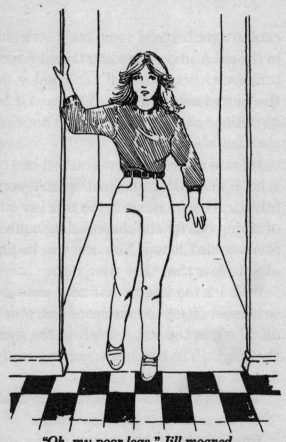

"Oh, my poor legs," Jill moaned.

night, Coach."

"Good night." Coach Remick looked at Jill for a moment. "Jill!"

Jill turned around.

"Good luck tomorrow."

"Thanks, Coach," Jill said. *I'm going to need it,* she thought.

The next day, Jill woke up aching all over. "Oh boy, I really overdid it last night!" she sighed. Most of the girls had only worked out for an hour or so. But Jill had worked for a full two hours. "Ouch!" Jill said as she bent over to put on her shoes. Her back was killing her. Walking down steps was even worse. "Oh, my poor legs!" Jill moaned as she limped into the kitchen.

Mrs. Palmer was setting some muffins and juice on the table. "Hi, honey, ready for the big day?" she asked.

"Oh, Mom, everything hurts—my

61

back, my legs, my arms. I overdid it at practice yesterday." She eased herself into a chair. "What am I going to do?"

"Let me see now. I think I still have some of that medicated cream your father used when he hurt his ankle. That's supposed to be good for sore muscles, too."

"You mean that smelly stuff he was always rubbing on his ankle?" Jill made a face.

"That's right. Do you want to try it?"

"All right," Jill said with a sigh. She started to get up.

"*After* breakfast," her mother said firmly.

Jill rubbed the cream wherever she had an ache or pain. It seemed to work pretty well. The only problem was that it smelled terrible.

At 3:00 P.M. sharp, she walked into

the gym. The tryouts started at 3:15. She looked around and gulped nervously. Half the junior class seemed to be there. She waved hello to some of the girls she knew. Then she walked over to Coach Remick and got a number.

"Remember, keep those legs straight," the coach said as she handed Jill number 45. "Just pin this number to your gym shorts and wait over there." The coach waved toward the far side of the gym.

Jill pinned on her number and joined the other girls. She tried to warm up, but it was too crowded to really stretch out.

"Quiet, everyone! Let me have your attention!" Coach Remick shouted. "We're going to start with a very simple cheer. We'll teach it to all of you. Then we'll split you up into small groups so that we can see all of you."

Coach Remick and another gym

She gave the cheer everything she had.

teacher, Mrs. Owens, taught the girls a short cheer. "V-I-C-T-O-R-Y, victory, victory, that's our cry!" Jill had seen the cheerleaders do this cheer many times. She knew all the movements by heart. And there were no cartwheels or other fancy tricks in this cheer. She breathed a sigh of relief.

The girls split into groups of ten. Each group would do the cheer twice.

As Jill's group got ready to do the cheer, Coach Remick gave them last-minute instructions. "Let's see a little more school spirit, girls!" she said.

That's one thing I've got, Jill thought. She gave the cheer everything she had.

Then Coach Remick called out the names of the girls she wanted to stay. "—and Jill Palmer. Will you girls please stay? The rest of you, thank you very much. We hope you'll try again next year." Jill had made it through the first cheer! She sat down with a big smile on her face.

Coach Remick taught the remaining girls a second cheer. This one was a lot harder. It had some tricky jumps, two cartwheels, and a handspring. Jill's heart started pounding. She watched Liz Hanley and some of the other girls breeze through the cheer. She was next.

Everything hurt terribly, but somehow Jill got through the cheer. She hoped her legs were straight. She finished and looked at the coach. Coach Remick and Mrs. Owens were talking quietly. Finally, the coach asked Jill to come over to them.

"Jill, what is your dress size? And how tall are you?"

Jill answered the coach. She was really excited. She must have made the squad!

The coach asked Jill to come over to them.

"Fine. Wait over there, please," the coach said, waving toward the bleachers.

At the end of the tryouts, ten girls were sitting in the bleachers near Jill.

"Jill, would you come here, please?" Coach Remick asked.

Jill hurried over to the coach.

"We've decided to offer you a special position, Jill. We like your school spirit, and you're just the right size to fit into our bear cub costume. How would you like to be the school mascot?"

Jill swallowed hard and stared at the coach in disbelief. "You don't want me to be on the squad?"

"We think you'd be a great mascot for the Bears," Mrs. Owens said. "It's a lot of fun. You get to do a routine of your own at every game. What do you say?"

Jill was quiet for a moment. "Was it my cartwheels?" she asked with a sigh.

"Well, Jill, let's just say that your spirit impressed us more than anyone else's," Coach Remick replied. "And school spirit is the number one requirement for the mascot."

Jill looked at the coach. "When can I try on my new costume?" she asked with a grin.

Best Friends

Cindy Talbot tapped her foot impatiently. She was waiting for her best friend, Donna Ross. The first day of school was over, and Cindy had so much to tell her! Donna was supposed to meet her in front of the gym at 3:30 P.M. It was 3:45 already. Cindy sighed. Donna was always late.

"Cindy!" Donna called as she ran down the hallway. "I'm sorry I'm late!"

"Boy, do I have to talk to you!" Cindy said with a secret smile. "Come on," she added, leading Donna toward the door, "let's not waste another minute!"

The two girls walked down the block to Jack's Diner. They sat in the back and ordered two Cokes and a plate of French fries.

"OK, Cindy, what's up?" Donna asked as she poured ketchup over her fries.

"Well," Cindy began in a low voice. She looked around to make sure no one else could hear her. "There's a new boy, Randy Harper, in my homeroom. He just moved here from Oakville. You should see him." Cindy rolled her eyes and sighed. "He has curly brown hair and big blue eyes. And he has the broadest shoulders! Oh,

*Cindy gulped and turned around
to face Randy.*

Donna, I think I'm in love!"

Donna looked at Cindy and laughed. "Boy, you don't waste any time, do you? When do I get to meet Mr. Wonderful?"

"I'll point him out to you at lunch tomorrow," Cindy said.

"It's a deal. Now can I tell you my bad news? I got stuck with old Mr. Norton for biology...."

The next day, Cindy and Donna walked into the cafeteria together. While they were waiting in the lunch line, Cindy looked around the cafeteria to see if she could spot Randy.

"Cindy!" Randy called, coming up behind her. "I didn't know you had lunch this period. Mind if I join you?"

Cindy gulped and turned around to face Randy. He was even better-looking up close. "Not at all," she said with a smile. "I'd like that." She looked at

Donna. "Randy, I'd like you to meet my friend, Donna."

"Nice to meet you," he said, holding out his hand. Donna smiled and shook his hand.

Cindy felt wonderful all during lunch. Randy had actually asked if he could eat lunch with her! He seemed to hit it off with Donna, too. Cindy was glad they got along.

After school that day, Cindy and Donna met at their usual place.

"Cindy, he is *gorgeous*!" Donna said with a sigh. "What a charmer! I'm so jealous that you saw him first!"

"I told you I have good taste," Cindy said with a laugh. "What would Doug say if he heard you now?"

"Doug who?" Donna asked jokingly.

"The one you were madly in love with this morning," Cindy said. "You do

74

remember him, don't you?"

"I'd rather not," said Donna with a laugh.

The next day, Randy sat next to Cindy in homeroom. He was friendlier than ever.

"That friend of yours is a nice girl," he said casually. "What did you say her last name was?"

"Ross," Cindy replied. She felt jealous of Donna for a moment. *That's silly,* she thought. *He's just being polite. Besides, Donna already has a boyfriend.*

Donna and Randy were standing together in the lunch line when Cindy walked into the cafeteria. As Cindy got closer, she gasped. Randy had his arm around Donna. Cindy was about to leave when Randy caught sight of her.

"Cindy, over here!" he said. Donna looked at Cindy with a guilty smile. "I'm just comforting your friend a little. Seems she had a rough time this morning," Randy said.

Cindy looked at Donna in surprise.

"Doug and I broke up," Donna said quickly. She didn't sound very upset about it.

"Oh, I'm sorry," Cindy said, looking closely at her friend.

Donna wouldn't look her in the eye. Why was she blushing? Could she and Randy be — ? Cindy pushed the thought out of her mind. Donna was her best friend. She wouldn't double-cross her like that. Besides, Randy didn't seem embarrassed.

The conversation at lunch was strained. When the bell rang, Donna jumped up and said she forgot something in her locker.

"Oh, Cindy," she added nervously, "I

can't meet you after school today. I have a dentist's appointment."

"OK, Donna. Talk to you later." Donna was acting very strangely. When Cindy called Donna that night, Donna seemed distracted.

"How was the dentist?" Cindy asked.

"What dentist?" Donna asked.

"*Your* dentist. I thought you had an appointment."

"Oh, that," Donna said. "OK. Listen, Cindy, I've got a lot of homework. I really can't talk now."

"All right," Cindy said slowly. "I'll see you tomorrow then."

After she hung up, Cindy sat back and closed her eyes. Something was wrong, but she couldn't quite put her finger on it. Donna never acted like this before. She'd talk to her tomorrow and find out what was the matter.

The next day in homeroom, Randy was very cool toward Cindy. He nodded hello and then ignored her for the rest of the period. "Randy," she began as they were leaving the room. "Are you—"

"Look, I'm in a hurry right now. I'll talk to you later," Randy said coldly. He looked past her and waved to one of his friends. Before Cindy could say anything, he had walked away. She was stunned. How could he be so mean? Why had he turned on her all of a sudden? Cindy choked back tears and hurried to her next class.

At lunch, Cindy looked around the cafeteria, but she couldn't find Donna or Randy. She waited in line with a sinking heart. Just then, she spotted Randy outside the cafeteria entrance. As he stepped aside, she saw that he had his arm around Donna. He bent down and gave Donna a kiss. Donna snuggled closer and gave him a playful hug.

Cindy was shocked. She couldn't take her eyes off them. The truth hit her all at once. Randy had only been using her to get to know Donna! And Donna had been lying to her all along! She wanted Randy for herself from the first moment she met him. Cindy felt sick. She walked out of the cafeteria in a daze.

Cindy was relieved that she didn't see Donna for the rest of the day. She needed time to think.

That night, Cindy called Donna on the phone.

"Donna, this is Cindy. I saw you and Randy in the hall today." Cindy took a deep breath. She was not going to let herself cry.

"I'm sorry, Cindy. I know you won't believe me, but I wasn't trying to take

*Cindy refused to speak to Donna
the next day in school.*

Randy away. It just happened," Donna said.

"You're right, I *don't* believe you. You're a liar, and Randy is the biggest phony I've ever seen. The two of you deserve each other. I hope you make each other miserable! I thought you were a friend, but I was wrong! You're my worst enemy. I'll never forgive you!" Cindy slammed down the receiver. She burst into sobs.

Cindy refused to speak to Donna the next day in school. Donna shrugged and stopped trying to talk to her. She was too wrapped up in Randy to think about anything else. She and Randy saw each other every day. Cindy avoided them as much as possible.

Two weeks later, Donna was waiting in front of Cindy's house when she came home from school. Cindy glared at Donna and tried to walk past her. Donna caught Cindy's arm and stopped her.

"Cindy, I didn't call because I knew you would hang up on me. Please listen to me for just a minute." Donna sounded very upset. She'd been crying.

"What is it?" Cindy asked coldly, shaking her arm loose.

"You were right, Cindy. Randy *is* a big phony. He broke up with me after his girlfriend in Oakville called me up and told me they were practically engaged!" Donna started crying. "Can you ever forgive me, Cindy? I've been so selfish and mean. I see that now. Are we going to let someone like Randy Harper break us up after all these years?"

Cindy had a lump in her throat. "I don't know," she said. "How can I trust you after what happened? What if another Randy came along?" she added bitterly.

"I would tell him to get lost," Donna said. "I want to get back with Doug—if he'll take me. I've been crazy these past two weeks! But I've learned my lesson. Please, Cindy, give me a chance to make it up to you!" Donna pleaded.

"You know, you can't erase what you did by acting nice," Cindy said quietly.

"I know. If only I could!" Donna said sadly. "I've missed you so much!"

Cindy looked at her old friend for a minute. "Let's go inside and talk about it," she said.

Why Can't You Be Like Your Brother?

Mrs. Stone filled up the water glasses on the dining room table. "Where is that boy? I've called him twice already!" She looked at Mr. Stone. He was reading the newspaper. "Harold, would you please *do* something! Mark doesn't listen to me anymore."

"Harold, would you please do something!"

"All right," Mr. Stone sighed, putting down his newspaper. "It's always something with that kid. Why can't he be like Larry?"

"I don't know. I can't understand it at all. Larry is such a good boy—and so smart. Everybody likes him. But Mark..." Mrs. Stone shook her head sadly.

"Mark is enough trouble for three kids, that's what, " said Mr. Stone. He was angry. He walked out of the room. "Mark, get down here this minute!" he shouted toward Mark's bedroom.

The door to the bedroom opened. "I'm not hungry," Mark called back.

"I don't care whether or not you're hungry!" Mr. Stone shouted. "If you don't get down here right now, you're going to stay in your room all weekend!" He went back to the dining room and sat down at the table. Mark came in a few seconds later. He sat down as far away from his father as possible.

"I expect you to listen to your mother, Mark. Is that clear?"

"Yeah," Mark said, staring at his plate.

"Good."

"We got a letter from your brother today," Mrs. Stone said with a proud smile. "He says he misses all of us. He's living in the freshman dorm, and he's made lots of friends there. He has a lot of homework, but he loves his classes."

"That's my boy!" Mr. Stone said with a big smile.

"Oh, and he joined the school tennis team," Mrs. Stone added.

Mark scowled and speared a potato with his knife.

"Watch your manners," Mrs. Stone

said with a frown. Then she started talking about Larry again.

Mark choked back his anger. All his parents ever talked about was Larry. "Larry is perfect. Larry is great! Why can't you be like Larry?" He thought things would get better after Larry went away to school. Instead, they got worse. He was sure his parents wouldn't miss *him* if he went away.

Mark started high school the following week. It was his first year at Lincoln High. His English teacher was taking attendance. "Stone, Mark."

"Here," Mark answered.

"Are you Larry Stone's brother?" the teacher asked.

"Yes," Mark said, gritting his teeth. Would he always be in his brother's shadow?

"Wonderful boy," the teacher said

with a smile. "One of my best students."

Mark's math teacher and gym teacher knew Larry, too. Mark was starting to feel desperate. The only class where he felt safe was shop. His brother never did any woodworking. Besides, Mark liked working with his hands.

Mark had a lot more homework now than he did in junior high. He had to write a paper for English, and he had math quizzes every Friday. And he knew his teachers were comparing him to Larry. He hated school. The only class he liked was shop. He was working on a cabinet for his stereo and records.

One night, while the Stones were eating dinner, the phone rang. "I'll get it," said Mrs. Stone.

When she came back into the dining room, she was frowning. "Mark, that was Mr. Thompson, your math teacher.

He said that you've been cutting class."
She paused for a moment. "He also said
that you're failing the course. Why,
Mark?"

"Why?" roared Mr. Stone. "I'll tell you
why! He doesn't care about anyone but
himself! He's trying to drive us both to
an early grave!" Mr. Stone was very red
in the face.

"Calm down, Harold! You're only making matters worse!" said Mrs. Stone.

Mark suddenly stood up. He was very
pale. "I feel sick," he said, running out of
the room.

"Not half as sick as you're going to
feel!" Mr. Stone shouted after him.

The next day, Mark was called into
the principal's office.

"Stone, I hear you've been cutting
English and math class. You come from
a good family. You should know better.

Your brother never got in any trouble at this school. I'm warning you. If I get one more bad report about you, I'll suspend you. Do you understand?"

"Yes, sir," Mark said, swallowing hard. Even the principal knew Larry!

"That's all, Stone," the principal said, dismissing Mark.

Mark stood staring out the window in shop class. Mr. Perry, the shop teacher, watched Mark for a minute. "Stone, see me after class," he said. The bell rang, and the room cleared out.

Mr. Perry walked over to Mark. "Stone, what's going on?" he asked with concern.

"Nothing," Mark said, looking at the floor.

"Nothing? Then why have you been cutting classes and trying to get yourself suspended?"

*"If I get one more bad report about you,
I'll suspend you."*

Mark looked at Mr. Perry in surprise. "How did you know?"

"The principal told all of your teachers to keep an eye on you."

Mark drew back. He was suspicious. Would Mr. Perry turn against him like everyone else?

"Stone, I'm worried about you. You're bright. You're one of the most talented woodworkers I have. So why do you hang out in the parking lot instead of going to classes?"

Mark turned away from Mr. Perry.

"Why throw it all away, Stone? You've got so much going for you."

Mark looked at Mr. Perry. Was he serious? "Tell my father that," he muttered.

"I think I will," Mr. Perry said with a thoughtful look.

That night at dinner, Mrs. Stone looked across the table at Mark.

"Mark, I got a phone call today. It was from Mr. Perry, your shop teacher."

"Oh no," Mark said under his breath.

"He said you were one of his best students. In fact, he wants to enter your cabinet in the school's industrial arts show." Mrs. Stone looked hurt. "You never mentioned anything about this to us," she added.

"I didn't think you cared," Mark said slowly, looking at his plate.

Mr. and Mrs. Stone looked at each other for a moment.

"Of course we care, dear," Mrs. Stone said gently.

"I'm really proud of you, son," Mr. Stone said. He leaned back in his chair. "You know, I made a bookshelf myself when I was in school."

"You did?" Mark asked in amazement.

"Sure. It's a great feeling, making

94

something with your own hands."

"That's just how I feel," Mark said. He couldn't believe his ears.

"I want to hear all about this cabinet," his father said, smiling at Mark.

The next day, Mark could hardly wait till shop class ended. When the bell rang, he went over to Mr. Perry.

"What did you tell my mother?" he asked.

"Only the truth," he said, smiling at Mark. "I told her that you're one of my best students and that I want to enter your cabinet in the industrial arts show. You'll probably be the only freshman in the show."

"Wow!" Mark said. "Do you really mean it?"

"I never say anything I don't mean, especially not to mothers," Mr. Perry said with a laugh. "I wanted to talk to your father, too, but he wasn't home. Did you tell him?"

"My mom did," Mark replied. "He said he was really proud of me. Do you know he once made a bookshelf himself? I never knew that before."

"I had a feeling he'd be pleased," Mr. Perry said with a wink. "There's only one problem."

"What's that?" Mark asked.

"You have to have at least a C average to be in the industrial arts show. You have a month to set things straight."

"I'll do it," Mark said. "And that's a promise."